# By Ginger Churchill
## Illustrated by Barry Gott

Tanglewood • Terre Haute, IN

Published by Tanglewood Press, LLC, October 2007.

Cover and interior design by Amy Alick Perich

Tanglewood Press, LLC
P. O. Box 3009
Terre Haute, IN 47803

Printed in China
10 9 8 7 6 5 4 3 2 1

ISBN-13:  978-1-933718-13-2
ISBN-10:  1-933718-13-7

*Library of Congress Cataloging-in-Publication Data*

Churchill, Ginger M.
  Carmen's sticky scab / by Ginger M. Churchill ; illustrated by Barry Gott.
      p. cm.
  Summary: Carmen has a sticky, oozy, crusty scab that she wants to pick, but everyone keeps warning her of the dangers--from infection to sharks--of scratching it.
  ISBN-13: 978-1-933718-13-2
  ISBN-10: 1-933718-13-7
  [1. Wound healing--Fiction. 2. Wounds and injuries--Fiction.] I. Gott, Barry, ill. II. Title.

PZ7.C47244Car 2007
[E]--dc22
                                    2007009893

Carmen had a scab. A sticky, oozy, crusty scab.

"Don't pick it," Mom said.
"It will get infected."

But the scab itched. Carmen picked it.

"Don't pick it," Dad said. "It will scar."
But the scab tickled. Carmen picked it.

"Don't pick it," Molly said. "If you bleed, sharks will eat you up."

Carmen tried not to pick it.

"Pick it," Andy said. "Scabs are delicious."

Carmen stayed away from Andy.

The edges of the scab curled up. Carmen rubbed it.
"Don't pick it," Miss Rawlins said. "Scabs grow new skin."

Carmen tried to think of something else.

"Don't pick it," the lunch lady said. "Germs will get inside."
Carmen held her scab on tight.

"It's starting to come off," Molly said. "Is there any blood?"
Carmen stuck it down with paste. And she watched for sharks.

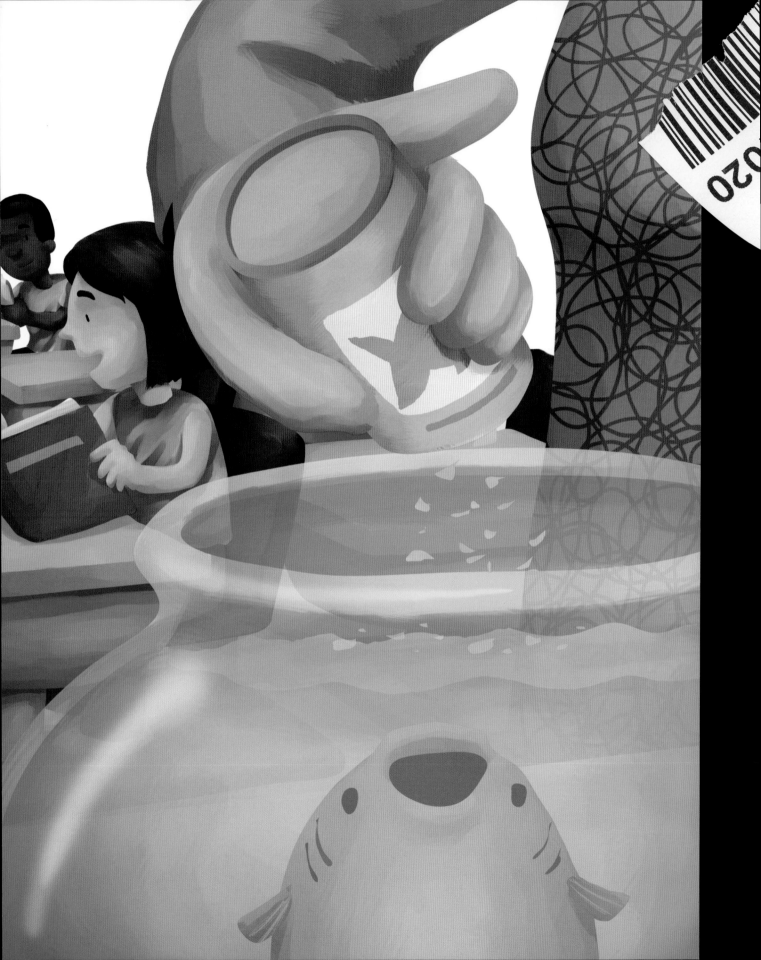

"Pick it," Andy said. "Don't you want to see
what's underneath?" He licked his lips.
Carmen ran away.

But the scab went wherever she did.

Carmen tried not to look at it. But she knew it was there.

"Don't pick it," the playground lady said. "It will hurt."
Carmen taped it down.

"Don't pick it," the bus driver said. "It could be messy."
Carmen scratched all around it.

"Don't pick it," Molly said. "We're going swimming tomorrow."
Carmen remembered the sharks.

"That thing's coming off!" Andy yelled.

He grabbed the tape and ripped
off the scab.
But there was no blood.

"Look at this," Carmen said. "I'm not bleeding."
Molly smiled.
"No more scab," Carmen said. "I'm all better."
The bus driver nodded.
Andy burped.

"It was delicious," he said.

THE END